CARRION LUGGAGE

SHANE SIMMONS

ISBN: 978-1-988954-02-8

Carrion Luggage
Copyright © 2003/2016 by Shane Simmons
All Rights Reserved.

Published by Eyestrain Productions
eyestrainproductions.com

Originally published by Vehicule Press in Island Dreams: Montreal Writers of the Fantastic, 2003; reprinted by Exter Press/Big Pulp in Black Chaos: Tales of the Zombie, 2014.

EYESTRAIN
PRODUCTIONS

THE TICKET SAID he was on a connecting flight out of Haiti to New York. There was a lineup of passengers for flight 207 to LaGuardia, and they all needed to be on board in the next ten minutes. The baggage checkers had to keep the pace brisk if they were going to stay on schedule. Still, they had to stop and look. He only had one bag with him and that would be easy enough to pass. There was just enough time to spare him a good lingering stare.

Florida's Panhandle International saw more than its fair share of oddballs and weirdos. Half the time they were also boarding a flight for New York.

This one was dressed like an undertaker, though not any undertaker of contemporary times. His clothes were black. Only the dress shirt under his vest and tie was a different colour: white. He had on an old top hat, dignified, but scuffed and worn by time.

His skin was almost as dark as his clothes, deeply coloured to the point where it nearly obscured the lines of his face in the poor lighting of the terminal. When his lips parted, the brilliance of his teeth drew the eye away from any less prominent feature. He smiled broadly. Too broadly. The smile didn't literally reach from ear to ear, but it came close, stretching right back to the hinge of his jaw as if his skin were too loose and his muscles too tight.

Margaret stood at her post next to the metal detector and waited for the man to approach. He looked down at her with yellow eyes magnified many times by the little circular glasses perched on the tip of his nose. The lens were almost as thick as they were wide with dozens of tiny air bubbles trapped inside the glass.

"Just the one bag?" Margaret asked.

"Only the one. Yes," he said, barely moving his lips and never breaking his unsettling smile.

Margaret broke his gaze and placed the bag on the conveyor belt. She watched it disappear through the flaps of the X-ray machine and then pointed the man towards the metal detector.

"This way please," she said, gesturing at the open doorway when he failed to proceed. He was still carefully watching the machine his bag had just disappeared into.

Attracting his attention with a broad wave of her arm, Margaret ushered the man through the empty frame of the metal detector. He had to duck to clear the top bar. He repeated the motion after tripping the alarm with a plain steel cigarette case the first time. It was the only metal item on his person, and he was cleared on the second pass.

Sally, the youngest member of the baggage-check crew, watched the X-ray monitor. She gasped loudly as the man came through to her side. It wasn't a reaction to him, although he might well have elicited a similar response had she been looking his way. She was staring at the monochrome outline of the contents of his bag.

"What the heck are those things?" said Sally, although she'd already taken an accurate guess.

Rob, her supervisor, looked up from the handbag of toiletries he was picking through. He was as surprised as Sally, but didn't let on.

"Looks like bones," he said matter-of-factly.

Everyone at the baggage check exchanged glances. Sally was still staring blankly at the screen, which was now exposing the more conventional contents of someone else's luggage. Rob caught the tall man's bag as it came through the second set of flaps and dragged it onto the counter. Everyone did their best to look over his shoulder from where they were already standing as he pulled it open. No one saw much, until Rob took out a darkened femur from the bowels of the bag for everyone to have a look at. The tall man watched the search carefully, but said nothing.

"That's a human bone, isn't it?" said Margaret.

"It can't be," Sally insisted.

Rob replaced it in the bag. When he withdrew his hand a second time, he had a human skull held carefully but firmly in his palm. Several gold fillings were clearly visible in the nearly complete row of teeth that hung down long and crooked. So was a wide fracture that spread across two of the skull plates in a jagged curve.

"My uncle," said the tall man in a tone that suggested he thought that would explain everything.

Everyone knew the flight was going to be delayed for sure now. The crew continued checking bags anyway as Rob telephoned security.

♦

Eventually they had to let the flight go, forty-five minutes late, with one seat empty.

The tall man sat in the airport security offices. He'd calmed down only after he was assured he'd be reimbursed for his ticket and put on another flight if everything was cleared in the next couple of hours. Since then, he'd been sitting perfectly still on a stiff wooden chair, with his hat in his lap. He'd offered no words or explanations since he'd handed over his passport. He just waited, politely.

Andrew Isaki returned to the desk where the tall man, identified as René Shanda on his passport, sat alone with only the video-surveyed door offering a way out. Andrew placed the passport on the desk and sat down on a couch across from Mr. Shanda. Shanda made no move to retrieve his documents. He sat expressionless, following Andrew with his eyes. There were answers to be had, and Andrew wasn't going to have an easy time of it.

It was Andrew's job to politely grill people detained from getting on a flight, usually until the appropriate officials arrived. He spent most of his time entertaining drug smugglers who were too stupid to know what kind of trouble they were in. Sometimes he was called on to testify in court, but not often enough to make the job interesting. Today's guest was an uncommon one. The police weren't on the way to take him off his hands. Not yet at least. Calls were still being made looking into the origin of what had turned out to be a complete adult male skeleton, cleaned of flesh, stuffed into one medium-sized travel bag.

"Mr. Shanda," Andrew smiled. Shanda didn't return his smile or greeting. Andrew tried again.

"I'm Andrew Isaki from airport security. I'd like to ask you a few questions about the contents of your bag."

Nothing.

"You said the bones in your bag were your uncle's."

"My uncle," confirmed Shanda.

"And what was his name?"

"Auguste Shanda."

"So," said Andrew, briefly considering how he could ask the next question casually. "What were you doing with his bones in your bag?"

"I was to take them to New York with me."

"Why's that?"

"Because that is where I am going."

"I see. Do you have any family there?"

Shanda hesitated a moment. "None living."

"You realize that it's generally considered…inappropriate for passengers to be carrying somebody's mortal remains on a flight, don't you? Airlines are happy to transport a body provided it's in a proper coffin in the baggage compartment. They do that all the time."

Shanda tipped his head slightly forward and looked at Andrew over his glasses like he was a fool.

"The bones are to stay with me always."

"I can understand your reluctance to entrust them to baggage handlers, but still…"

Andrew trailed off. He could see Shanda's point. A body touching down in Hawaii on the same day it's to be put to rest in Iowa is an embarrassment to all involved and just adds to a family's grief. Extra care is usually taken to make sure coffins go where they're meant to, but mistakes still happen. The Hawaii/Iowa rerouting had stirred up a fuss only three weeks earlier.

Andrew switched tracks. "Were you very close to your uncle?"

"Where are the bones now?"

"We have them securely stored. Don't worry."

"Securely stored" meant "sitting under the desk of a secretary who was off sick." The airport staff lockers were big enough for most personal valuables, but couldn't quite fit Shanda's bag. Andrew didn't want to try to stuff it in. He didn't know how brittle the bones were.

"Are you planning to bury your uncle's remains in the United States?"

Shanda said nothing.

"Are you relocating his body? How long has he been deceased, if you don't mind me asking?"

"He has been dead these past eleven days."

"Eleven days?"

Shanda fell silent again.

"That's a pretty advanced stage of decomposition for eleven days."

Shanda furrowed his brow, questioningly.

Andrew explained, "Why is he...why has he been reduced to bones already?"

"I boiled the flesh from them only yesterday."

He'd said it much as he might have explained that pants are put on one leg at a time.

"Why would you do that?"

"Easier to carry."

"Excuse me a moment, would you?" said Andrew as he got up. "Sure I can't get you anything?"

Shanda offered no suggestions, so Andrew left without another word.

◆

"I don't know, Bill," Andrew was saying five minutes later when he'd found Bill Mayer, his boss. "I don't know what local customs we could be dealing with here, but this sounds like some sort of weird serial killer racking up frequent-flier miles."

"Just give me the name, Andrew."

"He said it was Auguste. Auguste Shanda. Same last name."

"All right. I'll check with the Haitian authorities. See what they say. You just watch him."

"Come on Bill, do I have to? He'd not exactly a sparkling conversationalist."

"Think of it as a cultural gap. Bridge it."

"I prefer the Haitian weed smugglers. They're chatty."

"Bring him a soda and give him a sugar rush. That might do the trick."

"It's creepy, Bill."

"It's probably nothing. Don't worry about it. Remember last time this sort of thing happened and freaked out everybody?"

"Yeah, but that was an anthropologist sneaking out of Argentina with twenty-thousand-year-old fossils. It's not the same. At least we were pretty sure he didn't axe murder his cargo in the dead of night."

"This one's probably not a murderer either."

"Tell that to the guy with the cleaved skull."

◆

Andrew returned to his office to keep Shanda company until more calls could be made. He brought a diet soda for his guest and placed it on the desk, next to where Shanda was sitting. Shanda neither looked at the can nor acknowledged it being offered. Andrew took it in stride and sipped the foam off the top of his own opened can. He was getting used to the uncommunicative atmosphere in the room that day. When he sat down on the couch again, he drank quietly, neither looking at Shanda nor saying a word to him. When he finished his own drink, Andrew crumpled the can and accurately threw it across the room into the tin garbage can, where it clattered noisily. Only then did he look at Shanda once more. Shanda was staring back at him again, his attention drawn.

"How did your uncle die?" said Andrew casually once he'd regained eye contact

◆

Auguste Shanda had been the most feared *houngan* in all the villages that lined the shores of the Artibonite river in central Haiti. A high priest of a *houmfor* temple buried in the woods a mile back from the nearest road, he had been associated through rumour and hearsay with all the darkest dealings of voodoo lore. Presiding over traditional Saturday night ceremonies presented a legitimate front, but word spread through the towns and villages that on every other day of the week he was a *boko*, a sorcerer for hire, with no qualms about placing curses on friend or family for the right price.

The effectiveness of his doll curses was legendary, and it was well known he could cause anyone no end of misery with a wax-and-feather sculpture and as few as three of the intended victim's hairs—or a single toenail clipping. Folklore told of one occasion in Auguste's youth when he crossed paths with one of Duvalier's *Tonton Macoute*, a policeman and thug who dared challenge the Shanda family's authority in their own village. The number of physical ailments the officer endured thereafter was limited only to the number of needles in Auguste's mother's sewing kit. Within a month, the policeman ended his own suffering with a spectacular self-immolation by gasoline and Zippo in the middle of the town square. The method of suicide, few denied, may well have been connected to the fact that Auguste chose to dispose of the man's figurine likeness in a smouldering barbecue pit.

Auguste was also implicated in several high- and low-profile disappearances. His penchant for poisons was apparent, considering the number of his enemies who died in their sleep for no good reason. But the missing persons, insisted the townspeople in whispered tones, had likely been recruited as zombies. Auguste was an obvious suspect, considering the formula for the fabled zombie drug relied almost entirely on a poison thought to be understood by only a handful of boko—most of them now deceased, most of them by Auguste's hand.

The recipe for the poison included an elaborate mix of natural toxins and irritants that promoted swelling and severe itching. The intended victim would speed his own demise by scratching madly at an infected area until the skin broke. The poison, initially applied by sprinkling it on an arm or a leg while the marked man slept, would then infiltrate the bloodstream. A catatonic and highly suggestible state of mind would result within a few days, and the victim would become a zombie ripe for the picking, submitting himself to slavery at the hands of the first person who tried to command him.

Regular doses of the poison, administered by cut or pinprick, could keep a healthy adult in such a state for years. A boko of Auguste Shanda's skill was said to be able to extend a zombie slave's existence past any form of natural life, creating a living death of tireless, endless manual labour. The extra precaution of a doll curse might ensure the additional fear and loyalty needed to maintain control over a slave forever.

Such cruelty was not thought to be beyond Auguste Shanda. Put quite simply, nothing was considered beyond him. This belief in the scope and malice of his reach kept a dozen villages in a grip of fear so intense, it started to work against him. After so many miserable years under his thumb, people began to believe Auguste's reign of terror had to end some way. Any way.

René Shanda told Andrew none of this.

♦

"Andrew."

The call came from the door. Bill was looking in, waving him over. Andrew got up from his seat and walked over to Bill, who leaned in to whisper.

"Is he giving you any trouble?"

"He's not too co-operative," said Andrew, "but he's behaving himself."

"Think you can handle him on your own?"

"Sure, why?"

"I just got off the horn with Port-au-Prince police. Your friend Shanda there is wanted for murder. Guess who he killed."

"Oh boy."

"Yeah. A car's on the way from downtown, but the highway's packed with rush hour traffic. We've got him for another good half-hour."

"Okay."

"Packing?"

"Always."

"Good. I'll check in when the blue boys show up."

Bill dipped back out of the office, closing the door behind him. Andrew turned and saw Shanda staring intently. Andrew gave him a few moments of silence after he sat down again, then he spoke bluntly.

"Tell me why you killed your uncle."

Shanda answered immediately, calmly, like the question wasn't unexpected.

"You would not understand."

Andrew had convinced past guests to explain to him why they had tried to carry a gym bag full of hashish onto an international flight. Some had confided their reasoning for pulling a gun and shooting at state police who had them surrounded. He once even had a nineteen-year-old woman describe how she was coerced into carrying six latex condoms full of heroin in her stomach shortly before she died of an overdose when one of the condoms ruptured. The smuggling stories wore thin after a while. He never had anyone explain why they'd caved somebody's head in with a bladed weapon, though. He was hoping Shanda would level with him. Shanda didn't say much, but what he had said so far sounded true. If the tall man indulged him, Andrew was sure he would have a good story to repeat at this year's office party.

"Try me," said Andrew.

◆

Auguste Shanda's time on this Earth ended when he was quite old, but still strong of body and spirit. Despite the threat of an uprising from his fearful and superstitious flock, his finish came suddenly and unexpectedly when an anonymous road worker took a break from laying fresh gravel long enough to march into the foliage and cleave Auguste's skull wide open with his shovel. The worker thought he'd seen the high priest giving him the evil eye from the path that led down to his secluded temple and had panicked, daring a direct assault upon the voodoo sorcerer rather than risk the suffering of a prolonged curse. The irony was that Auguste had only come out of the woods to investigate the source of the noise caused by the idling city-works truck parked next to the series of potholes that needed filling. He hadn't given the worker any sort of eye, for good or ill—had never even seen him, in fact, right up to the moment of his murder.

The worker had returned to his home without saying a word to anyone. He didn't dare tempt fate by talking about his crime, even though he would have been hailed as a hero for it. It was up to René Shanda to discover the body of his uncle days later, when he first started to emerge from his poison-induced haze.

René, like so many members of the Shanda family, had served as a guinea pig for Auguste's potions as he evaluated dosages and adjusted his ingredients accordingly. They were considered expendable. Whether they died outright or became mindless zombie minions didn't really matter to Auguste as long as they helped him find the correct dose for paying clients.

René had proven to be a particularly successful zombie. Strong and agile, he'd been a real workhorse for the temple, clearing the jungle undergrowth as it encroached on the compound with each new rainfall. But he had also been an unusually willful zombie. A wax figurine of him had to be pricked and tortured routinely to keep him from wandering off or disobeying. Combined with the poison, it had kept René in check for years.

However, once there was no one to manipulate the doll or replenish the poison in his system, René began to wake up. He literally stumbled over Auguste's body as he walked through the woods, shaking off the last of his stupor. Another day went by before his head cleared enough for him to know what needed to be done.

René had been the only member of his family Auguste had bothered to keep at home. The rest—the ones who hadn't died outright from the poison—had been sold into bondage. There was a profitable demand for zombie labour among the Haitian-Red sects of Harlem. There were at least three restaurants operating in the north end of Manhattan that didn't need to pay their kitchen staff any wages. René had found out that a few of his closest relations numbered among the zombie dishwashers and floor-moppers. But before he could do anything about it, Auguste had made him his next victim.

Not that René had a plan back then.

He didn't know how the solution came to him. Perhaps in the years his conscious mind had been hidden away deep down inside, it still held enough of a spark to work on the puzzle. Ultimately, the answer was simple. René would make an antidote to bring to his enslaved family.

René knew just enough about Auguste and his perversion of voodoo rites to understand some of the principles behind his alchemy. He was sure, after dealing with poisons for so many years, Auguste must have built up a high tolerance to his own toxins. This immunity was in his blood, in his body, in his bones. The flesh was useless now—dead and rotting. But the bones could be recovered, the marrow dried and ground into a powder.

And the powder could be fed to his family.

That was the reasoning behind René's rapid departure from Haiti. He still had a passport, old and expired, but it could get him into America with enough tampering. A plane ticket was hastily purchased by selling off all of Auguste's possessions. By the time René was done pillaging his uncle's home, the only thing left of any value was an old cigarette case. René brought that along as his sole personal luggage, ready to pawn it for cab fare once he arrived in New York.

The last thing left to pack was Auguste's boiled bones. Only now did René realize he should have waited until they were dried and ground to dust before trying to transport them abroad. It was the one miscalculation he had made in his haste. That and leaving the rubbery stripped flesh of his uncle behind where police might find and identify it.

♦

"No," replied Shanda to Andrew's simple request.

"Why not?"

"I have said. You would not understand. You are not from the islands."

And that was the last thing Shanda had to say. Andrew tried to get something, anything, out of him for a few more minutes, but his guest had fallen into a meditative silence he couldn't cut through. He eventually gave up and resigned himself to the silent watch until the police came, passing the time by reading an airline magazine that was seven months out-of-date.

It only took twenty minutes for the police to arrive in the end. When they came, there were just two of them, neither detectives. They were there to transport Shanda to the feds in the city—glorified couriers, nothing more. Bill showed them in and the two uniformed cops cautiously set themselves at either side of Shanda. One of them had cuffs at the ready. The other had his hand on his holstered gun.

"Mr. René Shanda?"

Shanda didn't so much as look up.

"We're here to escort you downtown. We're placing you under arrest for the murder of Auguste Shanda, pending extradition to Haitian authorities."

Shanda didn't break the vacant stare he'd held since long before the police arrived. The only indication that he'd heard the officers at all was him holding his arms out in front of him, wrists together. The first officer snapped the handcuffs in place as the second recited Shanda's rights under American law. When the legal speech was done, Shanda stood, holding his hat in his cuffed hands, and let the officers lead him out, one on each arm.

No one could say how he spotted the bag on the floor when he was staring straight ahead the whole time. But suddenly, as they passed between the rows of office desks, heading for the exit to the terminal, Shanda pulled back sharply and broke the loose grip the cops had on his arms. The officers were slow to react, surprised by the sudden bolting of their formerly complacent suspect. Before they could turn, Shanda leapfrogged over the desk and landed on all fours next to his flight bag, which stuck out slightly from underneath it. The police had their guns drawn by the time he popped up again, grasping his luggage. They wasted a moment trying to tell him to freeze, but they probably wouldn't have been able to keep Shanda in place even if they'd fired at that moment or tried to jump him. He was moving fast, almost inhumanly so. He swung the bag wide, slapping both aimed guns out of his way with a sharp rattling of bones. In the same move, he stepped up on the table in front of him and was off, hopping from desk to desk as fast as a normal man might run across open land.

Shanda was out the door by the time the cops could get their guns pointed in his general direction. Neither of them fired. He was gone already, but they made chase.

Andrew and Bill followed the cops out. The police officers were waving people out of the way with their guns as they ran through the crowded terminal, leaving a clear path in their wake for the two airport security men. They knew there was no real danger, openly brandished guns or not. Shanda was unarmed, so there was no chance of a full-scale shootout. But he was giving them the best chase the airport had seen since three teenaged smugglers bolted from officers in three different directions a decade earlier. None of them had gotten as far as Shanda already had, dexterously bounding through business travellers, baggage carts, and sluggish tourists. The number of obstacles he had to detour around slowed him enough for the police, parting the crowd more easily with the sight of their guns and uniforms, to make up the distance.

Shanda might still have evaded his pursuers long enough to get outside and lose himself in the parking lot, if only he hadn't glanced back to check how much of a lead he had. In the second it took him to look over his shoulder, a baggage trolley stacked high with luggage headed home after a two-week Florida vacation appeared in front of him. He ran right into it and pulled the whole works down as he stumbled over the top. Suitcases popped open, sending cheap souvenirs and sandy bathing suits flying. Shanda's bag spilled its contents as well. No one had zipped it up since the search.

Half a dozen people were tripped up by the bones as they slid across the finely polished terminal floor. The skull landed right at the feet of a middle-aged woman fresh off the beach with a peeling sunburn and a Mickey Mouse hat to show for her travels. It took her a full second to realize what she was standing over, and another one to start screaming.

Screaming can disconcert a cop as easily as the next person and, after hearing the shrill panicked cries of the woman, one of them fired before thinking. As Shanda sat up suddenly, appearing behind the scattered pile of checked luggage, the lone bullet hit him mid-chest, slightly off-centre, and sent him lying back down again just as sharply. Both cops were still covering him from a distance when Andrew and Bill boldly stepped over the refuse.

Shanda was sprawled out, looking quite relaxed. His eyes were shut, and his glasses were tipped up across his hairline. He looked like someone's grandfather who had fallen into a light sleep on the couch between sorting through the sports page and the world news.

Bill opened his vest, looking for the gunshot wound. Not finding one, he immediately checked the inside breast pocket and pulled out what he suspected was there. The bullet had pushed through the first half of Shanda's sturdy cigarette case, but had flattened out on the second layer of steel. Loose tobacco from the destroyed stale cigarettes trickled out as Bill opened it to see the slug embedded inside.

"Lucky bastard. He'd be dead if..."

"He *is* dead," corrected Andrew who'd already taken Shanda's pulse twice, once at the wrist and once at the neck, and had come up with nothing both times.

"Can't be," said Bill.

"His heart's stopped."

"Call an ambulance!" ordered Bill. For the first time ever, he started using the CPR training he'd learned many years earlier.

He'd only pumped at Shanda's chest a few times before he stopped abruptly and felt the dead man's cheek.

"He's awfully cold for a guy who just sprinted halfway across the airport," said Bill.

"I know," agreed Andrew. "He feels like he's been dead an hour or so already. His fingers are getting stiff."

The crowd that had disappeared into the woodwork at the first suggestion of a shooting were gathering around again to see what sort of grisly results the gunplay had delivered. The ones who weren't busy discussing whether the bones where real human bones or not saw the next thing that was pulled out of Shanda's inside breast pocket. It was a doll, like a toy, but uglier than anything anyone would ever give to a child. It was crude and barely recognizable as a human icon, made more grotesque by the ragged hole in its torso where the policeman's bullet had torn through on its way to striking the cigarette case.

"I don't think he bought that at the souvenir shop," said Bill.

Andrew wasn't listening. He studied the face of René Shanda, who had died only moments ago and now looked like a corpse exhumed after a month in the ground. He was wondering how best to word a report to the FAA that wouldn't get him fired.

END

ABOUT THE AUTHOR

Shane Simmons is an award-winning screenwriter and graphic novelist whose work has appeared in international film festivals, museums and lectures about design and structure. His art has been discussed in multiple books and academic journals about sequential storytelling, and his short stories have been printed in critically praised anthologies of history, crime and horror. He lives in Montreal with his wife and too many cats.

ALSO BY
SHANE SIMMONS

Novels

Necropolis
Sex Tape
Filmography

Short eBooks

Choke the Chicken
Hot Pennies
The Red Baron: An Ace for the Ages

Graphic Novels

The Long and Unlearned Life of Roland Gethers
The Failed Promise of Bradley Gethers
The Inauspicious Adventures of Filson Gethers

LAST WORDS

Small-press publishers rely on reviews from readers like you to help get the word out about their books. Whether it's a simple star rating or a written critique, every bit of feedback helps convince the impersonal computer algorithms of Amazon, and other literary outlets, that the book you just read has merit and deserves more exposure. Please support independent authors, editors and publishers by taking a few moments to share your thoughts and opinions with other potential readers who may be sitting on the fence about trying an intriguing novel or collection. Your suggestions or comments can make all the difference when it comes to helping them find a new writer they'll like, or matching a struggling author with the readership he or she deserves. Thank you.

www.ingramcontent.com/pod-product-compliance
Lightning Source LLC
Chambersburg PA
CBHW020323150626
46552CB00022B/3194